CHOCOLATE SPAGHETTI...

FOR BREAKFAST

ESPAGUETIS DE CHOCOLATE

PARA EL DESAYUNO

Written by Debra R. Sanchez

Illustrated by Laura Garvin

Tree Shadow Press

Tree Shadow Press
www.treeshadowpress.com

ISBN: 978-1-948894-17-3

DEDICATION

For those who said,
"Write a title you'll never write a story for...
then write that story."
I did.
Thank you for the prompt.

Para aquellos que dijeron,
"Escribe un título para el que nunca escribirás una historia...
entonces escribe esa historia".
Lo hice.
Gracias por el reto.

I'm awake,

but Mom's asleep

Estoy despierta,

pero mi Mamá no está

and I want to fix my own food.

y quiero hacerme comida.

I don't want to wake her,

No quiero despertarla,

Even though I probably should.

Aunque sé que debería.

I'll sneak to
the kitchen

and not make a sound.

Iré a la cocina sin hacer ningún ruido.

I'll look in the 'fridge.

Miraré en la nevera.

Oh, what's this I found?

¿Qué hay escondido?

I can't find the sauce,
but here's leftover spaghetti.

No encuentro la salsa,
pero hay espaguetis de sobra.

I don't want it dry,

but I'm hungry already!

No los quiero secos,

pero tengo hambre ¡ya!

What will I do?

¿Qué puedo hacer?

What's that I see?

¿Qué veo aquí?

Some chocolate syrup

Sirope de chocolate

for my spaghetti!

¡Para mi espagueti!

I feel someone looking.

My mom just woke up.

Alguien me mira.

Mamá se despertó.

She looks kind of green
seeing spaghetti and syrup.

Su cara se ve verde.

viendo espagueti achocolatado.

I offer her some.

"Just take a taste."

Le ofrezco un poco.

"Prueba una bocada."

"Well maybe a little, so it won't go to waste"

"Tal vez un mordisco así que no se botará."

She opened her mouth,

and just took a bite.

Ella abrió su boca,

y mordió un poquito.

Then she smiled and said,

"You know, this is alright."

Ella sonrió
y dijo,
"Sabes, esto
está rico."

So, when she sleeps late,
and I'm up already,
I can always just make
some chocolate spaghetti.

Ahora, si ella duerme tarde,
y yo me levanto,
puedo hacerme
espaguetis con chocolate.

ABOUT THE AUTHOR

Debra R. Sanchez has moved over thirty times and has lived in five states in two countries...so far. She and her husband have three adult children, five grandchildren, and a dog and a cat. She leads writing groups, workshops and retreats. Her writing has won awards in various genres, including children's stories, poetry, fantasy, fiction, and creative nonfiction. Several of her plays and monologues have been produced and published. Other works have been published in literary magazines, newspapers, and anthologies.

Debra R. Sanchez ha mudado más de treinta veces... hasta ahora. Ha vivido en cinco estados en dos países. Ella y su marido tienen tres hijos adultos, cinco nietos, y también una perra y una gata. Ella dirige grupos, talleres, y retiros para escritores. Su escritura ha ganado premios en varios géneros, incluyendo cuentos infantiles, poesía, fantasía, ficción, y no-ficción creativa. Varias de sus obras de teatro y monólogos han sido producido y publicado. Otras obras han sido publicadas en revistas de la literatura, periódicos y antologías.

And My Mother Cried / Y Mi Mama Lloró was awarded "Best Children's Book of 2017" at The Author Zone (TAZ) awards. *Prompted, Prodded, Published: How Writing Prompts Can Help All Writers* also received a 2017 TAZ award in the non-fiction category. *Raw & Unfinished*, received a TAZ award in 2018 for poetry. Her play *Pages: A Library Play (Páginas: Un Cuento de Bibliotecas)* was published in 2016 in both English and Spanish.

For more information, visit her webpage:
Para más información, visita a su página web:
www.DebraRSanchez.com
Follow her on Facebook:
Síguela en Facebook: @DebraRSanchez

ABOUT THE ILLUSTRATOR

Laura Garvin is an illustrator and dreamer who has a passion for drawing cute characters and colorful scenes. She lives in Pittsburgh, PA with her cat Blueberry.

Laura graduated from Youngstown State University and when she isn't drawing she loves hiking and exploring the city.

Even though she's never tried chocolate covered spaghetti, Laura doesn't think it sounds too bad.

Laura Garvin es una ilustradora y soñadora a la que le apasiona dibujar simpáticos personajes y escenas coloridas. Vive en Pittsburgh, PA, con su gato Blueberry.

Laura se graduó de Youngstown State University y cuando no está dibujando le encanta ir de excursión y explorar la ciudad.

Aunque nunca ha probado los espaguetis cubiertos de chocolate, Laura no cree que estarían tan mal.

For more information, visit her webpage:
Para más información, visita a su página web:
https://www.snailberryart.com/
Follow her on Social Media:
Síguela en Medios Sociales: @snailberryart

Made in the USA
Middletown, DE
09 June 2021